WALT DISNEY PRODUCTIONS
presents

PINOCCHIO
AND THE ISLE OF FUN

Random House New York

First American Edition. Copyright © 1984 by Walt Disney Productions. All rights reserved under International and Pan-American Copyright Conventions. Published in the United States by Random House, Inc., New York, and simultaneously in Canada by Random House of Canada Limited, Toronto. Originally published in Denmark as PINOCCHIO I SLARAFFENLAND by Gutenberghus Gruppen, Copenhagen.   ISBN: 0-394-86535-9 Manufactured in the United States of America   4 5 6 7 8 9 0   A B C D E F G H I J K

Geppetto the woodcarver
was a kindly old man who
loved children.

But he had no children
of his own.

So he made a puppet
that looked like a boy.

A kitten and a fish
lived with Geppetto
too.

One night Geppetto looked at
the wooden puppet.

"I will call you Pinocchio,"
Geppetto said. "How I wish you
were alive!"

Pinocchio was
silent.
He was only
a wooden doll.
Geppetto yawned
and went to bed.

The kind Blue Fairy heard
Geppetto's wish.
She liked Geppetto.

So she waved her magic wand
over Pinocchio.
The wooden puppet came alive!

Pinocchio ran to Geppetto.
"Look!" Pinocchio called.
"I can talk and walk!"

"My wish has come
true!" cried Geppetto.
He hugged Pinocchio.
They were so happy!

"Now you are
a real boy,"
Geppetto said
to Pinocchio
the next day.

"You must go to school. You will learn
to know right from wrong. You will learn
to be brave and to tell the truth,"
said Geppetto.

"I'll make you
proud of me!"
Pinocchio said.

Pinocchio ran down the path to school.
Geppetto hoped Pinocchio would do well.
Sometimes it was hard to be brave.
Sometimes it was hard to tell the truth.

Pinocchio had no worries.

He skipped along and sang a happy song.

"Oh, I'm as happy as a boy can be,

because there are no strings on me!"

Two sly fellows heard Pinocchio's song.
"Ha!" said J. Worthington Foulfellow
to Gideon Cat. "That's the boy for us!"

The mean old fox
put out his foot and
made Pinocchio trip.
Down tumbled the boy!

"Oh, dear me,"
said Foulfellow.
"I'm sorry! I hope
you're not hurt."

The fox picked up Pinocchio and dusted
him off.

"Where are you off to, my fine lad?"
asked the fox with a smile.

"I'm going to school," said Pinocchio.
"I must learn to know right from wrong,
to be brave, and to tell the truth."

"Those are all good things to learn,"
said J. Worthington Foulfellow.

"But it's such a beautiful day! You should sing and dance and have fun outdoors today," the fox said.

He and the cat twirled the boy around.

"You should visit the Isle of Fun!" they said to Pinocchio.

"I can't," said Pinocchio. "Geppetto—"
"I'm sure that Geppetto wants you
to have fun," said Foulfellow. "Look,
that coach will take you to the seashore.
You can get a ship there. It will take you
to the Isle of Fun."

The big coach was filled with boys.
They were laughing and shouting.
A jolly coachman stood nearby.
A team of donkeys pulled the coach.

"I guess I can start school tomorrow,"
said Pinocchio.

Pinocchio climbed onto the driver's seat.

He did not see the coachman give money to the fox and the cat.

He did not see that the little donkeys looked sad and tired.

Pinocchio did not know right from wrong. All he thought of was the Isle of Fun!

A boy sat next to Pinocchio.

His name was Lampwick.

"Stick with me," Lampwick said. "What a good time we'll have!"

Soon the coach began to move.
The coachman whipped the donkeys.

The donkeys pulled the heavy coach
down the long road to the seashore.
   There lay the ship.
   It was ready to sail to the Isle of Fun.

The coach stopped.
"Here we are," said the coachman.
The boys raced up the gangplank.

Pinocchio knew he should
not go on the ship.

He should go to school!

"Hurry up!" Lampwick said.

He pushed Pinocchio
up the gangplank.

Soon the ship arrived at the Isle of Fun.
The boys could hardly wait to go ashore.

There were all kinds of rides and games.
There was a circus with animals.
There was even an orange juice river!

Pinocchio and Lampwick rode around and around on the merry-go-round.

They ate
ice cream.

They shot at targets.

"Don't choose
just one dessert.
Eat them all!"
Lampwick said.

Suddenly the coachman appeared.
He did not look jolly anymore.
He cracked his long black whip.

"Right this way, lads! Time to pay
for your fun," the coachman called
to all the boys.

The boys started to run away.
But what was happening?
The boys did not look just like boys.
They began to look like little donkeys!

"Run, Pinocchio!
Save yourself!"
called a donkey
with long ears.
He was wearing
Lampwick's clothes.

Pinocchio's ears were long and furry too.
And he had a tail—just like a donkey!

Pinocchio ran away as fast as he could.
Soon he came to the edge of a high cliff.
"Stop!" cried the coachman.

Pinocchio did not want
the coachman to catch him.
So he dived right into the sea—
SPLASH!

Pinocchio swam through the cold water.
"I should have gone to school today!"
Pinocchio cried. "Then I would not be
in such trouble. I want to see Geppetto
again. I want to tell him
how sorry I am."

The waves tossed Pinocchio up and down.

Finally the sea washed him
up onto the shore.
Pinocchio fell asleep,
all worn out.

After a while Pinocchio woke up.
He still had his donkey ears and tail.
But he was alive!

"I must find my way home," Pinocchio said.
"This way!" twittered three kind birds.
So Pinocchio set off.

It was a long walk.
Rain fell.

The rain
turned
to snow.
The snow
grew deep.

But Pinocchio bravely trudged on to town.

After many hours Pinocchio reached
his town.

It was dark and cold.

"I must tell Geppetto why I look
like this," Pinocchio said sadly.

The Blue Fairy
suddenly appeared.
"You are brave
and truthful now,"
the Blue Fairy said
to him. "You know
right from wrong."

She touched Pinocchio with her wand.
POOF!
His long ears and tail were gone!
Then the Blue Fairy disappeared too.
Pinocchio knocked on Geppetto's door.

Geppetto opened the door.

"You've come home!" cried Geppetto.

"Yes—and I promise to be a good boy from now on," said Pinocchio.

He and Geppetto hugged each other.

Everyone in Geppetto's house was merry
that night!